The Perfectly HORRIBLE Halloween

Nancy Poydar

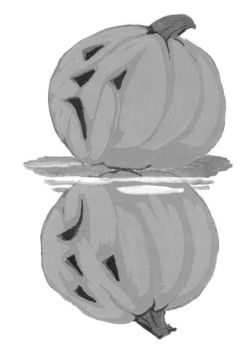

HOLIDAY HOUSE / New York

Copyright © 2001 by Nancy Poydar
All Rights Reserved
Printed in the United States of America
www.holidayhouse.com
The text typeface is Lucida.
The artwork was created with pencil and gouache.

Library of Congress Cataloging-in-Publication Data
Poydar, Nancy.
The perfectly horrible Halloween / Nancy Poydar..
p. cm.
Summary: Fearing that his Halloween at school
will be ruined because he has left his pirate outfit
on the bus, Arnold uses his imagination to come up
with a new costume.
ISBN 0-8234-1592-9 (hardcover)
ISBN 0-8234-1769-7 (paperback)
[1. Costume—Fiction. 2. Halloween—Fiction.
3. Schools—Fiction.] I . Title.
PZ7.P8846 Pe 2001   00-039675
[E]—dc21

For
Henry

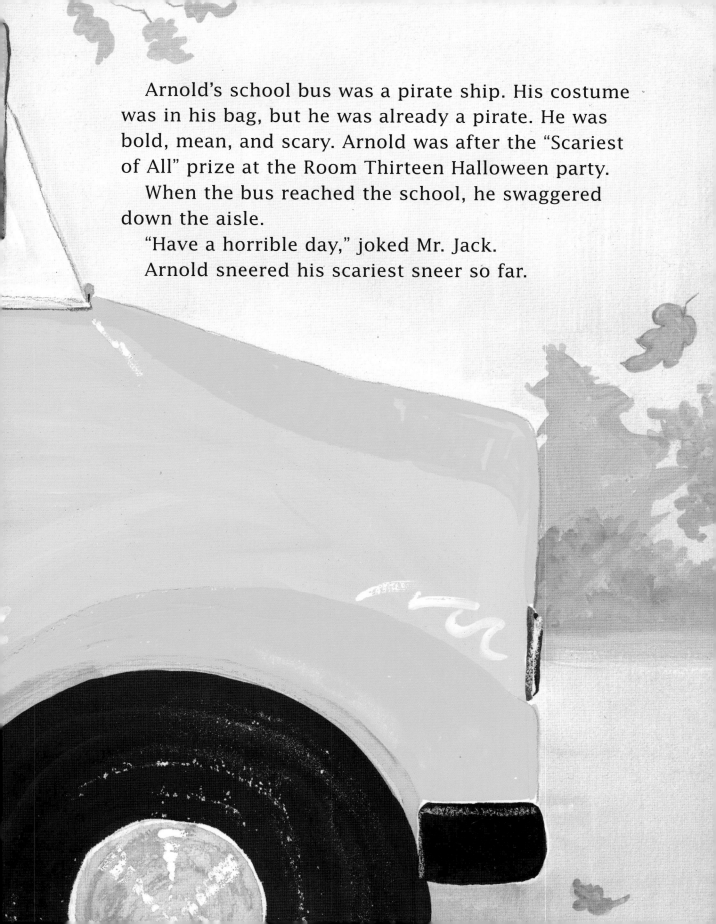

Arnold's school bus was a pirate ship. His costume was in his bag, but he was already a pirate. He was bold, mean, and scary. Arnold was after the "Scariest of All" prize at the Room Thirteen Halloween party.

When the bus reached the school, he swaggered down the aisle.

"Have a horrible day," joked Mr. Jack.

Arnold sneered his scariest sneer so far.

Mr. Roche said it would be business as usual until the end of the day. Then they would have the costume parade and prizes.

"I'm going to be a pirate," boasted Arnold. "I have chocolate gold coins for everybody. I'll have bushy eyebrows and a beard and a tarantula tattoo!"

"Horrible," exclaimed Harriet. "Horrible!"

Arnold just knew he would be scary enough for the "Scariest of All" prize. It would be his pirate treasure!

Arnold thought about his chocolate gold coins. He thought about his costume.

He went to his cubby just to *look* at them.

He pushed aside his jacket and a sweater. He found five pencils. He found two dead bugs from last week's show-and-tell. There were lots of papers but no pirate things.

He looked in the cubby beside his.
He looked in the cubby on the other side.

Where was that bag?

"Oh, no!" Arnold remembered just where his chocolate gold coins were. He knew just where his beard and eyebrows were, and his bandanna, his sword, his earring, his eye patch, his parrot, and the tattoo. He had left them on the bus! He *was* going to have a horrible day.

"Spelling," announced Mr. Roche.

"*Spooky,*" he dictated. Then came *ghost* and *scary. Eerie* and *pumpkin* were next. *Horrible* was for extra credit.

"Arnold, you're not listening!" scolded Mr. Roche.

Arnold was feeling *horrible*. If I were a pirate, he thought, Mr. Roche would walk the plank!

"Arithmetic," said Mr. Roche. "Put your answers in the pumpkins."

Arnold thought Mr. Roche looked like a pumpkin. Maybe *I* could be a pumpkin, Arnold thought, but he couldn't figure out how. Pumpkins didn't scare him, anyway, and he wanted to be "Scariest of All."

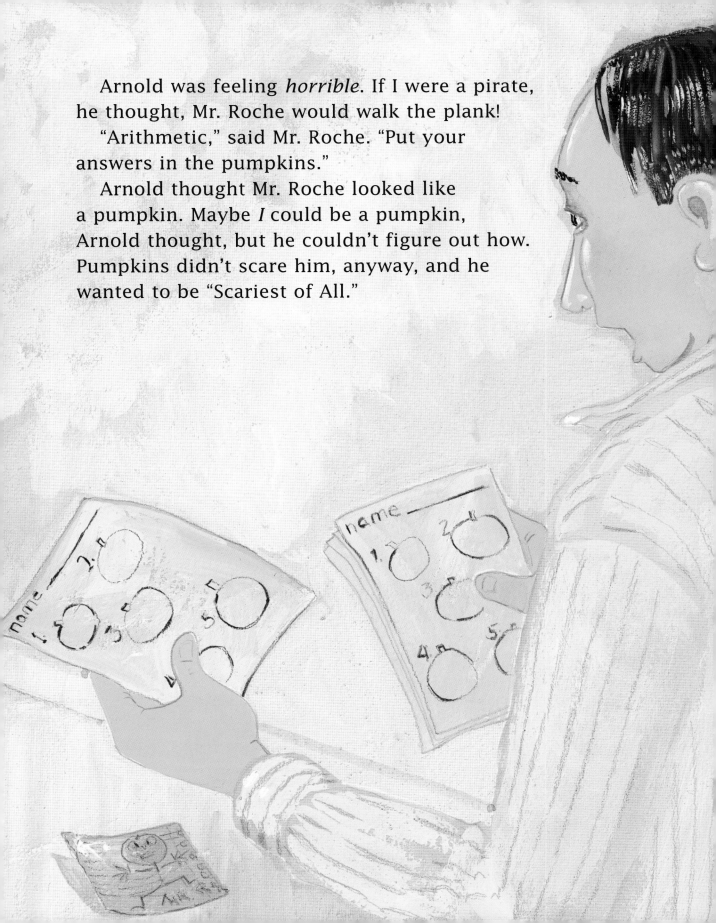

Finally, Mr. Roche said it was costume time. The class began to change. Arnold wanted to change, too.

He put his jacket on backward. He put
his sweater on, too. He let the arms dangle. He had
two legs and four arms. He noticed their World of
Bugs mural. He stuck pencils in his hair. He was a
bug! A scary bug!

"Bzzzzzup. Bzzzzzzup. Zup. Zup."

A headless horsewoman pranced over. "It's not time to go home yet, Arnold," she said.

A wizard touched Arnold's antenna with a magic wand. "Why are you wearing pencils?" he asked. One fell to the floor. Arnold felt bad.

He put his clothes back.
He tried to stuff himself into his cubby.
If only the wizard could make him vanish.
Where could he hide? Then he spied
the cloth they'd stood on when they
painted their mural.

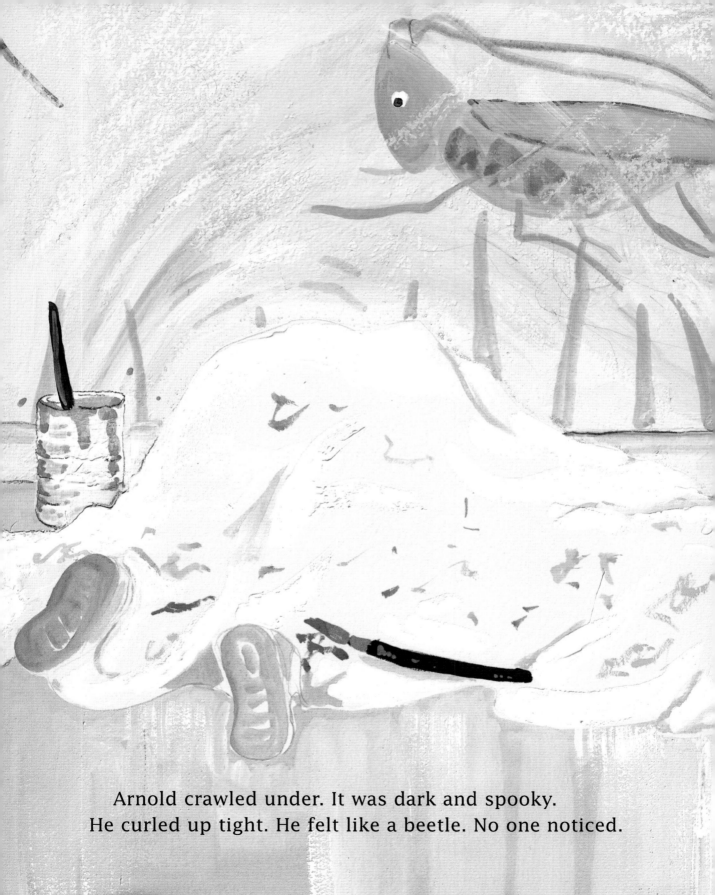

Arnold crawled under. It was dark and spooky.
He curled up tight. He felt like a beetle. No one noticed.

He could hear everyone getting ready for the party.

"Cupcakes for everybody!" That was Princess Harriet.

Arnold's chocolate gold coins would have tasted better.

Swish. Swish. That was Wizard Walter's magic wand.

Arnold's sword would have been more frightening.

"Giddy-up!" That was Suzanna, the headless horsewoman.

Arnold, the pirate, would have been much scarier.

It was eerie and sad to hear what was going on and not be seen. Arnold the Invisible, he thought.

"Arnold?" Mr. Roche's voice interrupted the buzz.

"Where's Arnold?"

"He's disappeared," whispered the wizard.

"He's a ghost," hissed the headless horsewoman.

"How horrible!" declared the princess.

"Look in the bathroom, Walter," said Mr. Roche. " Look in the hall, Suzanna."

"You can't see ghosts," warned the headless horsewoman.

"Arnold's not a ghost," said Mr. Roche. "He's just disappeared temporarily."

A ghost, thought Arnold. That's what I am, a ghost! I'm eerie, spooky, and SCARY! His hand crept over and tapped the princess on her royal ankle.

Eeeeeeeeek!

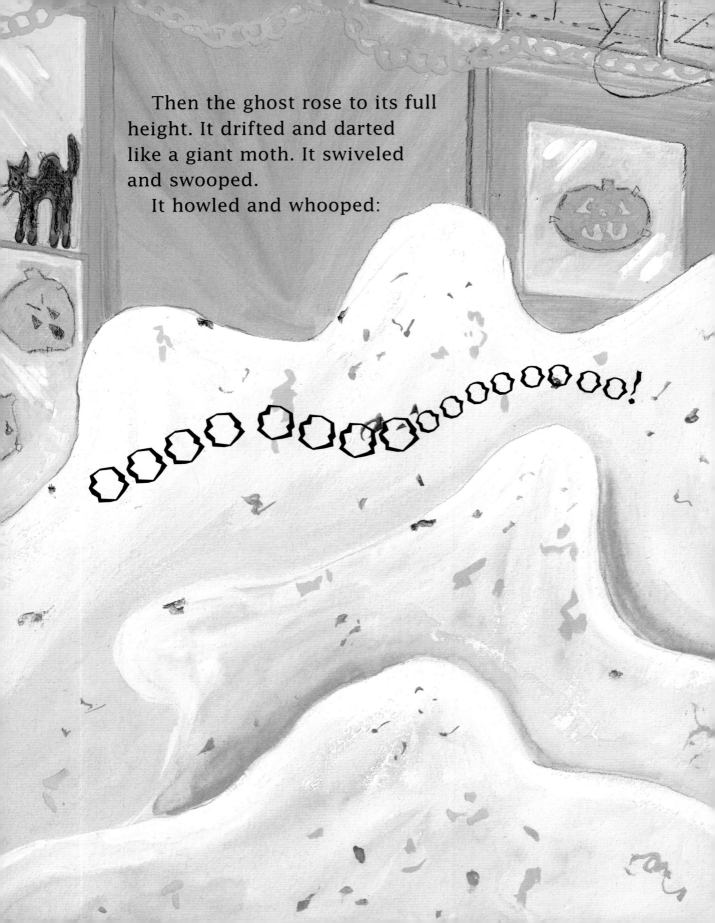

Then the ghost rose to its full height. It drifted and darted like a giant moth. It swiveled and swooped.

It howled and whooped:

OOOOOOOOOOOOOOOOOOOO!

It frightened the wizard and made
the headless horsewoman drop her head:
BUMPITY, BUMP, BUMP.
It even startled Mr. Roche.

"Arnold?" guessed
the clown and
Mother Goose.

"Arnold?" wondered the wizard.

"Arnold is the scariest of all!" declared Mr. Roche.

"You really were horrible," said Harriet. "But what happened to the pirate?"

Mr. Jack snickered. "All aboard, mates," he said. "And anyone who is too noisy will walk the plank!"